How to Catch a Falling Star

Written by Heidi Howarth
Illustrated by Daniel Howarth

"What are you doing?" asked Hedgehog.

"Sitting and waiting for the star to fall," replied Bear grumpily. "The last star of the year."

"Oh. Can I wait, too?"

Bear said nothing. He just shuffled
along to make a space.

And they sat and waited.

"What are you doing?" asked Mouse.

"Sitting and waiting for that star to fall," replied Hedgehog and Bear, pointing high up into the treetop.

"Oh. Can Rabbit and I wait, too?"

Bear and Hedgehog said nothing. They just shuffled along to make a space.

And they sat and waited.

Squirrel had been watching
from high in the treetops.
He had a wonderful idea.

"Don't worry, I can get it
down for you," he called.

He reached out his paw...

"No!" cried Bear, Hedgehog, and Mouse.

Rabbit was too shy and said nothing.

"Don't touch it!" said Bear. "If you touch it, the magic will be lost."

Squirrel stopped.

"What magic?"

"Very strong magic,
but not if you touch it!"
shouted Bear.

Squirrel looked closely. The leaf
looked the same as all the other
leaves he had seen on the tree.

Squirrel scampered down the tree and rummaged through a pile of leaves.

"What is he doing?" asked Bear.

"I can't see," said Mouse. "I'm too small."

Bear smiled for the first time.
"Sit on my shoulder if you like."

Mouse was surprised.
"Thank you," he said.

No one noticed Squirrel scampering back up the tree. Now he sat there with a leaf in his hand.

Silently, he dropped it.

Bear gasped, Hedgehog shook,
Mouse squeaked, and they all
watched the leaf fall.

"We have to catch it,"
called Bear.

"We have to catch
the magic."

But where had it gone?

Still, no one had noticed Squirrel.
Suddenly his little tummy shook
as he let out a big chuckle.

They all looked up.

"It's right there," chuckled Squirrel.

"Behind you!"

Bear turned around,
but the leaf wasn't there.

Mouse and Rabbit turned around,
but the leaf wasn't there.

Hedgehog turned around,
but he couldn't see the leaf either.

Suddenly Bear, Rabbit, and Mouse started to laugh.

"The leaf's not behind you. It's on your behind!" they cried, pointing to the leaf on Hedgehog's prickles.

Bear looked sad.

"What's wrong?" asked Hedgehog.

"The magic is gone, and I needed it," cried Bear.

"But what for?" asked Mouse.

"To wish for someone to play with." Bear started to cry.

"Is that all? You have us, silly!"
cried Hedgehog, Mouse, Squirrel,
and even Rabbit.

And with that, the five friends
played together every day.